This book is given with love...

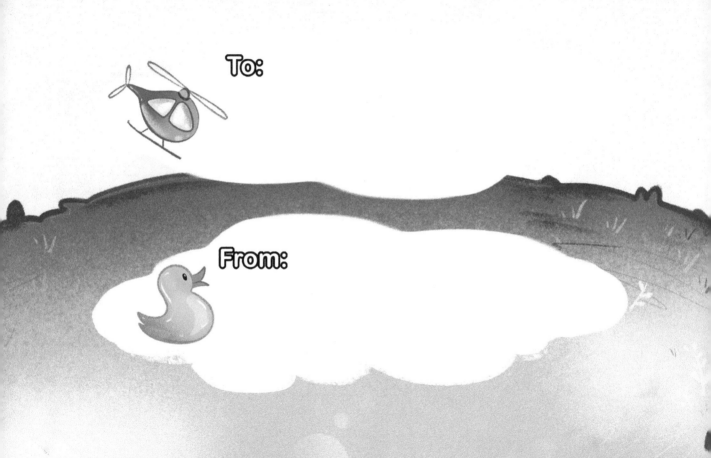

To:

From:

Foreword
Dr. Haitham Ahmed

As our little ones grow and learn, they start to become attached to the material things around them. Feeling possessive over their new belongings is natural, so it becomes our responsibility to teach them the joy of sharing with others. Sharing is challenging at first, but can be mastered with slow and patient practice.

In this book, children learn how to tackle feelings of greed and over-consumption, express gratitude for what they have, and pay attention to the feelings of others.

Through fun rhymes and thoughtful examples, this book teaches children how to overcome the challenges of sharing, succeed in making friends, and how to become constructive, cooperative citizens of this world that we all share.

For all inquiries, please contact us at:
info@puppysmiles.org

To see more of our books, visit us at:
www.PuppyDogsAndIceCream.com

For kids that want EVERYTHING...

Do I Need More?

Illustrated By
Jenny Yevheniia
Lisovaya

Written By
Dr. Haitham Ahmed

The world around us is filled with joys,
So many new and exciting toys!
Action figures, kites, and board games,
Big stuffed animals with funny names.

Tea sets, balls, and colored blocks.
A moving robot that beeps and talks,
Dolls, bikes, and so much more,
Each aisle is magic in the store!

You see commercials on TV,
You think "That toy is meant for me!"
When passing shelves where toys are stacked,
It's hard to put what you want back.

It's natural to desire it all,
When at the toy store or the mall.
The colorful boxes look so bright,
So many treasures in plain sight!

You feel the longing in your chest,
To have those toys would be the best!
The "want" you feel can build and build,
You ache to have that want fulfilled.

But wait a second, let's look back.
Instead of all the toys you lack...

Just think how many things there are,
Almost as many as the stars!

Each thing you want will take up space,
Because every toy will need its place.

**To buy a toy takes time and cash,
You fill your room and make more trash.**

Instead of wanting everything,
See all the joy that each toy brings.

When things are harder to come by,
Their worth can grow with short supply.
A treasure's greater when it's rare,
And more valuable when it is shared!

Everyone has got a spark,
That makes them light up in the dark.
Your passion builds just like a flame,
When others join you in a game.

Share your gifts, your brain, your skills,
You'll help each other climb the hills.
No mountain peak will seem too high,
When you're a team, aim for the sky.

Appreciate all the things you own,
Nothing's fun when you're alone.
When you share more among your friends,
You'll like the way the story ends.

If everyone can open hearts,
We're greater than our separate parts.
There isn't time or space for greed,
When we all share, there's less we need.

You learn from others when you share,
Build new skills, and friends see you care.
Your interests may expand and grow,
There's lots of stuff that others know.

When sharing is the thing you do,
Others want to be with you.

When you're open with your toys,
Friendship follows and so do joys.

Connections form when you share tasks,
If you need help, go on, just ask!

Solo ants don't build their hills,
Instead they all combine their skills.

Time to wear your thinking hat...
When you last shared, how great was that?
Perhaps you gave a friend your snack,
Next time you asked, they shared theirs back.

You helped a teammate on the field,
They scored a goal, their skill revealed!
Did it feel good to give a lot?
Remember now, when you did not...

Remember when you didn't share,
You played alone. No one was there.
You kicked a lonely soccer ball,
Against a quiet, old brick wall.

Perhaps you got a brand new bike,
Remember what that day felt like?
A giant smile lit up your face...
Until you found no one to race.

When you work hard
for things you earn,
They make you happy
in return.

If something's easy,
soon it's passed,
And that enjoyment
may not last.

Too many things create a big mess,
You may like things more when you have less.

Appreciate each gift you get,
Don't sweat the ones you don't have yet.

Gratitude impacts us all,
For both the big things and the small.
Share your joy and share your stuff,
And soon you'll find – you have enough!

When we are thankful for our gifts,
We'll find that our perspective shifts.
Share with others, go explore...
Once you start giving, you'll have more!

Claim your FREE Gift!

Visit 🐾

PDICBooks.com/Gift

Thank you for purchasing

Do I Need More?

and welcome to the Puppy Dogs & Ice Cream family.
We're certain you're going to love the little gift
we've prepared for you at the website above.

CPSIA information can be obtained
at www.ICGtesting.com
Printed in the USA
LVHW072306240423
745254LV00020B/134